Surprise in the Sand

A MAX, MIA, AND TOBY ADVENTURE

Written by Tennant Redbank
Illustrated by Celestino Santanach

Max and Mia flipped through postcards at Destination Station.

"Here's one from Zahra," Max said.

"I miss her," Mia said. "I wish Egypt weren't so far away."

"I wonder what she's doing right now," Max said.

"Look!" Mia cried. "The postcard!"

Max smiled. He knew just what to do. Destination Station was a special place.

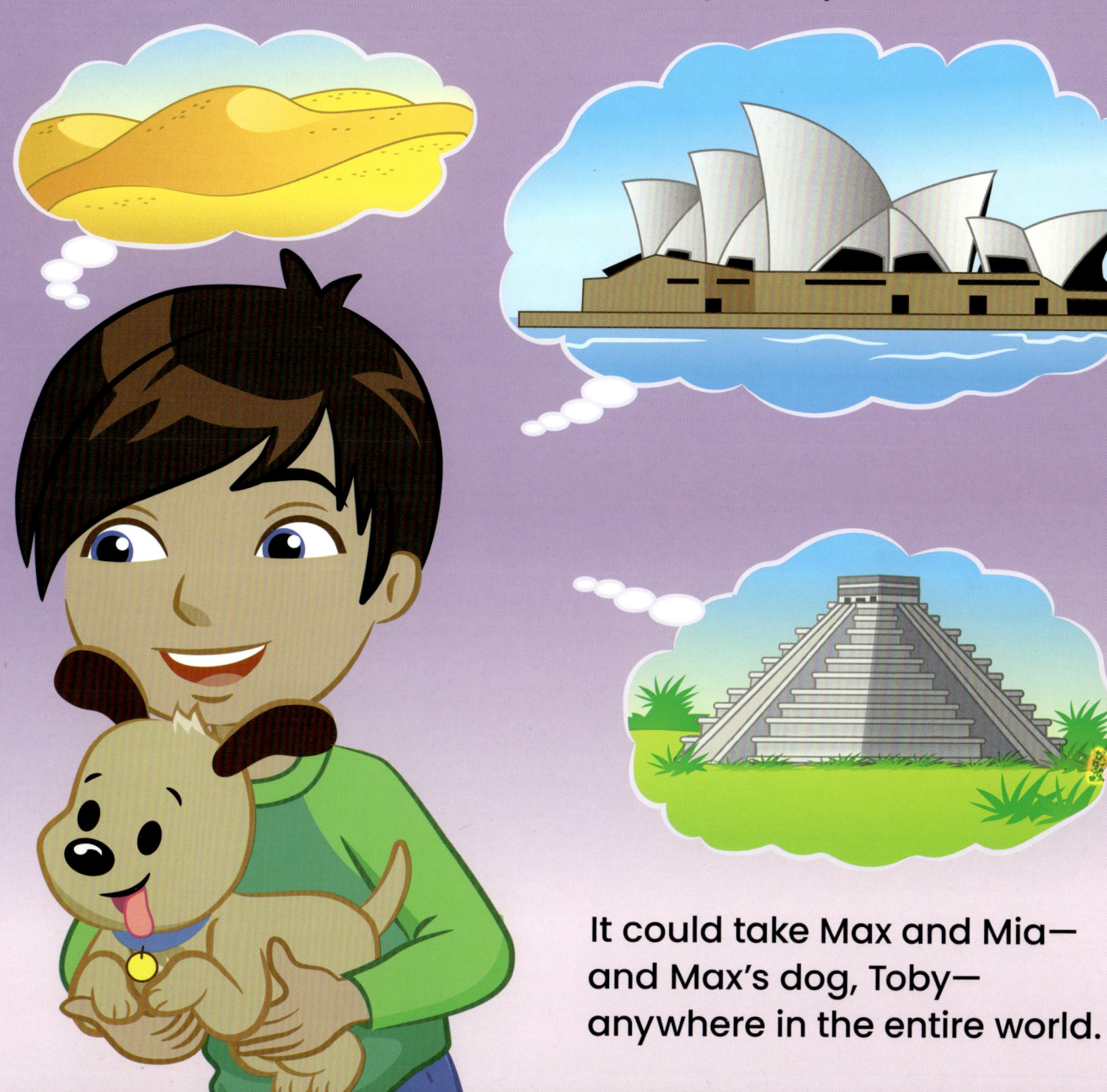

It could take Max and Mia— and Max's dog, Toby— anywhere in the entire world.

Max rang the bell.

Mia spun the wheel.

"Places to visit, new things to know," they sang. "Our postcard is stamped. We're ready to go!"

Max and Mia ducked into the slide, with Toby right behind them.

They landed in sand, sand as far as they could see.

Destination Station had done it again.

They were in **Egypt!**

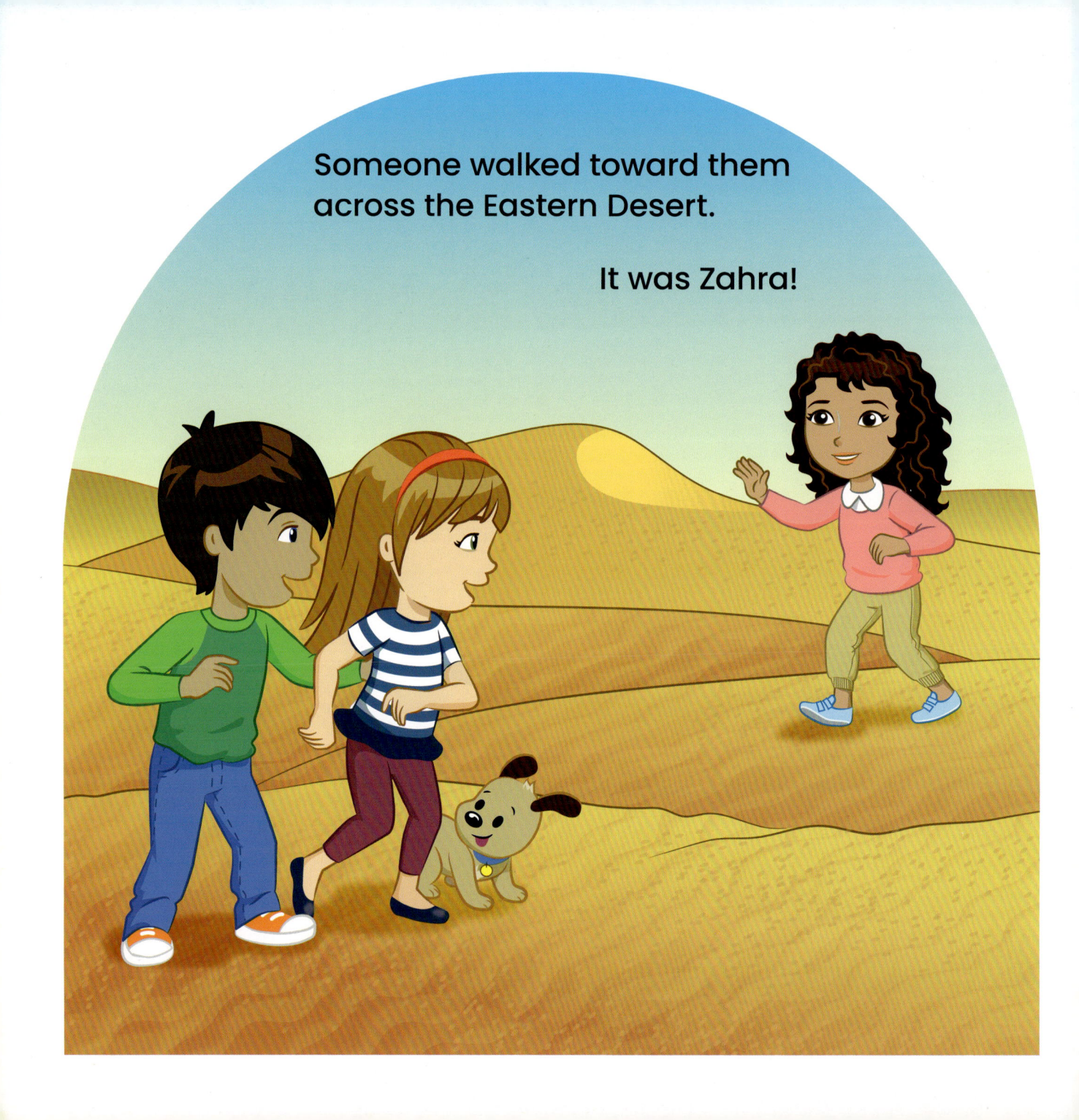

Someone walked toward them across the Eastern Desert.

It was Zahra!

"I was just thinking about you," Zahra said. She had a big smile on her face.

Mia laughed. "We were thinking about you, too!"

"Woof!"

The friends turned to watch Toby digging in the sand. He had sand in his fur . . . and something in his mouth!

Toby dropped it for Max. "Did you find a sandal?" Max asked.

"I wonder who it belongs to," Mia said.

"Let's find out!" Zahra said. "Hooray! A puzzle to solve!"

A band of travelers passed by. They were going to Cairo.

Each person had two sandals, not just one.

"Maybe the sandal belongs to someone in Cairo," Zahra said. "It's the biggest city in Egypt."

"Let's go!" said Max.

Zahra led them to a Cairo bazaar, a perfect place to find handmade items.

"If you lost a shoe, you could buy a new one here," she said.

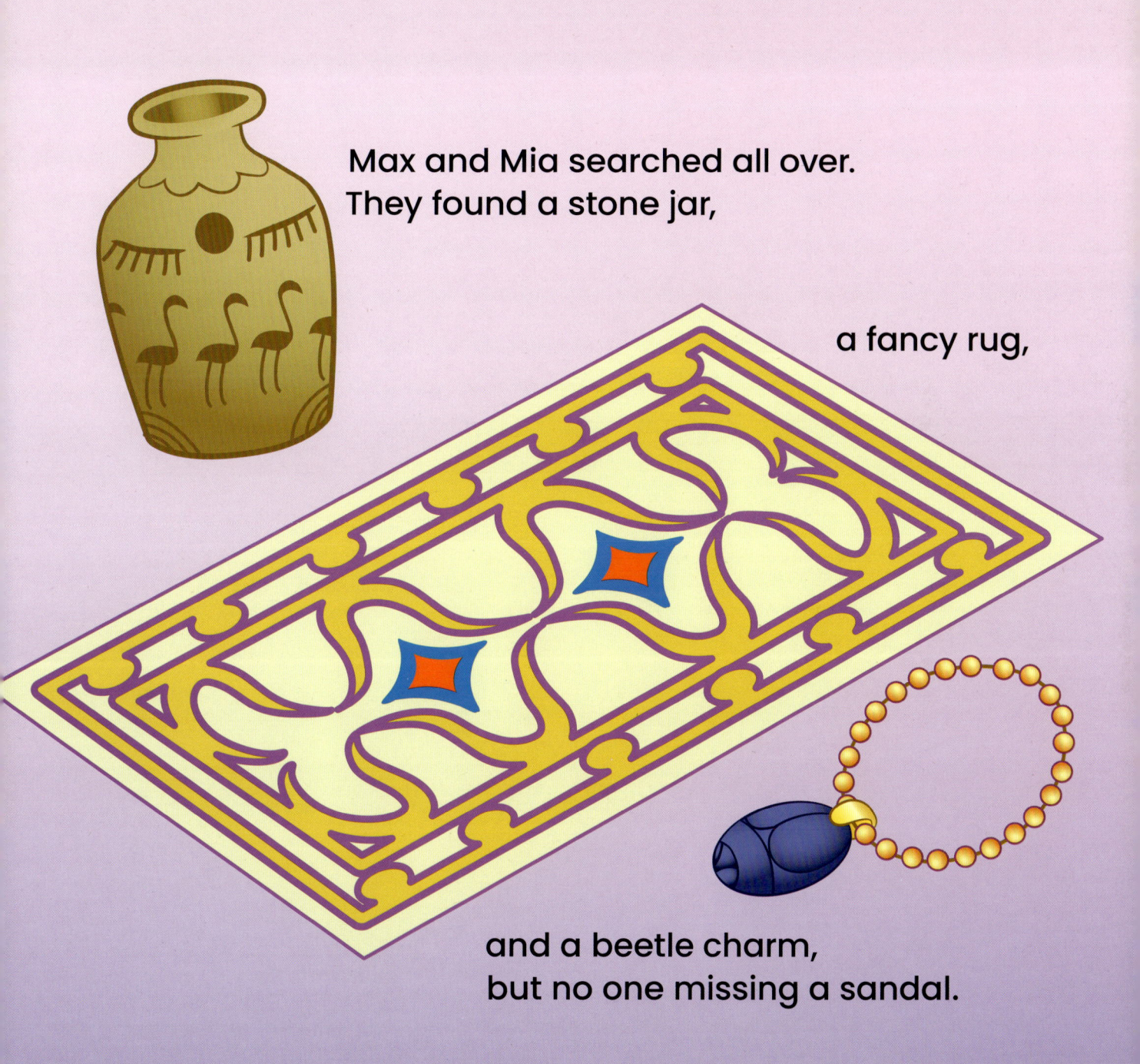

Max and Mia searched all over.
They found a stone jar,

a fancy rug,

and a beetle charm,
but no one missing a sandal.

"Maybe we should look along the river," Mia suggested.

"Good idea," Zahra said. "Everyone comes to the Nile. Captain Babu will help us search from his felucca."

Max, Mia, Toby, and Zahra climbed aboard the boat. They looked along the banks and on the other boats passing by.

Everyone wearing sandals had a complete pair.

"The pyramids of Giza!" Max said.
"They're super popular to visit.
 I bet someone there lost the sandal."

The pyramids rose high above the sand. Max's and Mia's eyes moved up, up, up the towering structures pointing to the sky.

"I never knew they were so big!" Mia said.

"Egyptian rulers were buried in those pyramids," Zahra explained. "And their treasure was buried there, too!"

Max and Mia checked everyone's feet, near the pyramids and by the stone Sphinx statue.

No one's sandals were missing.

At last, the kids sat down in the shade of a tent. A group of people were digging nearby.

"I give up," Max said, the sandal in one hand. "We'll never solve this puzzle."

A woman in a big hat and a blue shirt overheard him. "That's quite the find!" she said.

Her name was Dr. Hassan, and she was part of a team of archaeologists. Archaeologists uncover history—one artifact at a time.

Dr. Hassan studied Toby's sandal. "It looks like it might be three thousand years old!" she declared.

Max, Mia, and Zahra stared at each other with wide eyes and open mouths.

"My dog dug it up," Max told Dr. Hassan.

"It usually takes A LOT more work to dig up an artifact," Dr. Hassan said. "And many more tools!"

"Oh, Toby!" Mia said. She, Max, and Zahra laughed. Toby looked very proud of himself.

Max and Mia gave the sandal to Dr. Hassan. It belonged in a museum.

"We solved the puzzle!" Zahra said.

"Of course we did," said Max. "And now Toby's treasure has a new home."

Max and Mia looked at each other.
"Home," Mia echoed.

They knew it was time to go.
Max pulled the postcard from his pocket.

"Thanks for the adventure!" Mia said.

"I'll write soon!" Max promised.

"Woof!" added Toby.

Zap!

Ding!

Zing!

In the blink of an eye, Max, Mia, and Toby were home again!

Max smiled at Mia. "I wonder . . . where will we go next time?"